Collect 5 tokens and get a free poster!*

All you have to do is collect five funky tokens!
You can snip one from any of these cool Bang on the Door books!

 0 00 715297 3

 0 00 715309 0

0 00 715307 4

 0 00 715308 2

 0 00 715305 8

**Send 5 tokens with a completed coupon
to: Bang on the Door Poster Offer**

PO Box 142, Horsham, RH13 5FJ (UK residents)

c/- HarperCollins Publishers (NZ) Ltd,
PO Box 1, Auckland (NZ residents)

c/- HarperCollins Publishers, PO Box 321,
Pymble NSW 2073, Australia
(for Australian residents)

 0 00 715306 6

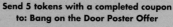

Title: Mr ☐ Mrs ☐ Miss ☐ Ms ☐ First name: .... Surname: ....

Address: ....

....

....

Postcode: .... Child's date of birth: ...... / ..... /

email address: ....

Signature of parent/guardian: ....

Tick here if you do not wish to receive further information about children's books ☐

LP01

I token

Terms and Conditions: Proof of sending cannot be considered proof of receipt. Not redeemable for cash. Please allow 28 days
delivery. Photocopied tokens not accepted. Offer open to UK, New Zealand and Australia only while stocks last. *rrp £3.99

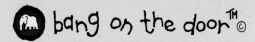

bang on the door ™ ©

little princess joins in

Collins

An imprint of HarperCollinsPublishers

Little princess looked in the mirror and admired her perfect purple dress, her perfect pink shoes and her sparkly crown and wand.

"Perfect!" she said, smiling
at her royal
puppy dog.

Little princess was so pleased that she went for a ride on her shiny purple bike.

la la la la
la la la l

She sang happily as she cycled along.
Of course, she had a perfect singing voice.

Just then, **ballet girl** came twirling by.

She twirled so fast that she made
a great big cloud of dust and mud!

What a mess **little princess** looked!

There was mud
on her pretty
dress...

and dust
on her
shiny bike.

Her perfect
hair was all wrong,
and even her
sparkly crown had
fallen off!

"My precious
royal things!"
cried **little princess**.
"It simply won't do."

Little princess was cycling along...

...just as **little sweetheart** watered her lovely flowers.

"My precious royal things are all wet!" she sobbed. "It simply won't do. I'm going home," she sighed sadly.

On the way home she saw...

little sweetheart sliding down a shiny slide...

and **ballet girl** bouncing on a trampoline.

It looked such fun that **little princess** forgot to be sad and began to giggle!

"Would you like to play with us?" asked little sweetheart.

"But they're already
all messy!" cried **ballet girl.**
Little princess looked at
her dusty bike, her mucky
dress and wobbly crown
and wand.

It was the best fun
she had ever had!
"Oh my," said **little princess**,
"look at my perfect
royal things!"

"They're still perfect!" giggled little sweetheart. "A perfect mess!".

First published in Great Britain by HarperCollins Publishers Ltd in 2003
1 3 5 7 9 10 8 6 4 2
ISBN: 0-00-715309-0
Bang on the door character copyright:
© 2003 Bang on the Door all rights reserved.
🌀 bang on the door™© is a trademark
Exclusive right to license by Santoro
www.bangonthedoor.com
Text © 2003 HarperCollins Publishers Ltd.
A CIP catalogue record for this title is available from the British Library.
The HarperCollins website address is: www.fireandwater.com
Printed and bound in Hong Kong